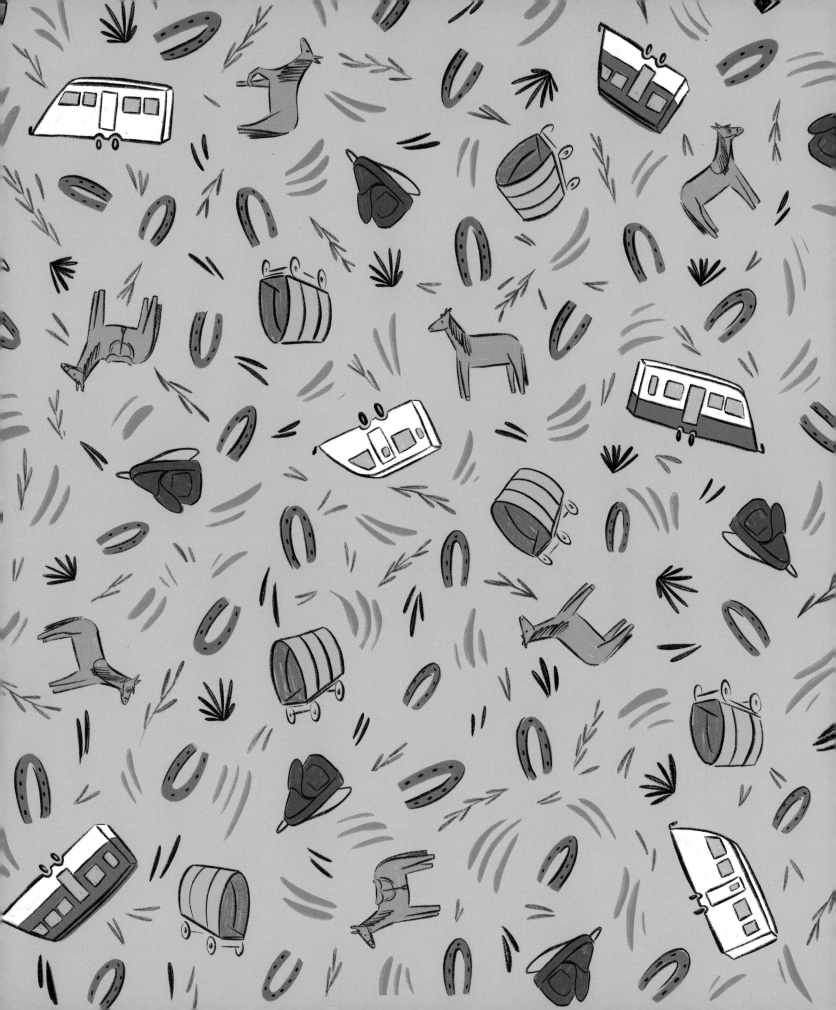

To Tommy and Grandma Lou-Lou

Richard

First published in 2019 by Child's Play (International) Ltd
Ashworth Road, Bridgemead, Swindon SN5 7YD, UK

Published in USA in 2019 by Child's Play Inc
250 Minot Avenue, Auburn, Maine 04210

Distributed in Australia by Child's Play Australia Pty Ltd
Unit 10/20 Narabang Way, Belrose, Sydney, NSW 2085

Text copyright © 2019 Richard O'Neill
Illustrations copyright © 2019 Child's Play (International) Ltd
The moral rights of the author and illustrator have been asserted

ISBN 978-1-78628-346-7
WP150319CPL05193467

Printed and bound in Guangdong, China

1 3 5 7 9 10 8 6 4 2

A catalogue record of this book
is available from the British Library

www.childs-play.com

Glossary:

Kushti atchin tan: *Good stopping place* - **Driving gry**: *Horse experienced at pulling carts*

Bitti mush: *Little man* - **Kushti**: *Good* - **Jall-on**: *Move quickly* - **Vardo**: *Traditional horse-drawn wagon*

The LOST HOMEWORK

RICHARD O'NEILL

ILLUSTRATED BY

KIRSTI BEAUTYMAN

Sonny lived on a Traveler site with his parents, cousins, and other neighbors. The site was a kushti atchin tan, a real community, and there was always something going on.

Sonny loved school. He liked to do his homework on Friday so that he could enjoy the weekend without having to think about it.

This particular Friday he was busier than usual as the family was going to a cousin's wedding the following day.

The cart had to be cleaned ready to transport the newlyweds.

Shoes needed to be polished, and clothes
had to be put out ready for the morning.

They had to call the farrier because Lollo the driving gry had thrown a shoe. The farrier heated up the metal shoes until they were glowing red, orange, and then white.

"Why do they have to be so hot?" Sonny asked.

"To create what's called thermal expansion," she explained. "The metal's structure changes when it reaches 2,372 degrees Fahrenheit, so I can adjust the shape of the shoes to fit the horse's hooves."

Later that evening, Sonny got out the road map to plan
the journey. He liked being able to picture where
they were going. Besides, the last time
they'd used the GPS it had taken
them the wrong way!

"We'll have the horsebox
and the trailer, so remember to
avoid the highway," said Dad.

Sonny wrote down the route, and used the scale to calculate the distance.

"So," said Dad, "if the wedding is 112 miles away and we drive at 50 miles per hour, it will take us..."

"At least 2 hours and 15 minutes," calculated Sonny.

Early next morning they set off wearing their best clothes.

Uncle George and Auntie Pearl led the way, with Sonny reading the map. The rest of the family followed behind.

When they arrived, Lollo was harnessed to the cart to take Bettie-Leigh to the church. After the service, the newlyweds traveled to the reception together.

Mom and Dad chatted with family and old friends.
"Oh look, there's Great Aunt Regina," said Sonny,
rushing over to say hi.

After the meal and the speeches,
there was music and dancing.

Sonny hovered by the stage, holding his harmonica.
He wasn't much of a dancer but loved playing music.

"Up you come, bitti mush," said the singer.
"The more kushti musicians the merrier!"

Later, the storyteller took to the stage. After sharing a few tales, he asked if anyone else wanted a turn. Sonny was a little nervous but worked up the courage to perform his latest story. The crowd laughed and clapped.

"That was a great story," the storyteller said. "Where did you learn it?"

"I wrote it at school," Sonny replied.

The storyteller smiled and nodded. "Well done."

As Sonny and his family got ready to head home, they could hear the storyteller and some of the older people still telling their tales.

Before church on Sunday, Sonny took the younger children to the park.

"Let's see who can do the fastest circuit," Crystal laughed. "Jall-on!"

"We're not supposed to get our Sunday clothes dirty," said Sonny.

After church, Sonny stopped in at one of the bungalows near the site. "I'm glad you're here, Sonny," said Mrs Stevens. "I want to email my grandson. I'm sure you can show me how."

"Of course!" replied Sonny.

"Goodness, when I was your age we had to find a pen, write a letter, and mail it... then wait days for a reply," laughed Mrs Stevens.

"Life might have been a lot easier with one of these," Sonny smiled.

Sonny loved cooking, so when he got home he rushed to help his mom with the Sunday dinner. She said he made the best popovers in the world.

All of a sudden he remembered that he still hadn't done his homework. But his book wasn't in his school bag. It wasn't in his bedroom either. He even looked in the truck, but it was nowhere to be seen!

Panicking, Sonny ran back to his mom.

"I can't find my homework book!" he cried. "Can you help me look for it?"

"I'm putting out the food, Sonny," said Mom. "I'll help you look for it later. Don't worry, there's plenty of time."

After lunch, Sonny had offered to help his local community group. Grandma had given them her old vardo, and they were restoring it.

"We need to finish the painting today," announced Shirley, the leader.

"Look at these old pictures I found," said Sonny.

"Wow, look at the detail," said Gary.
"Whoever painted that caravan was very talented."

On his way back to the site, Sonny remembered his homework again.
"Can you help me find my homework book, Aunt Pearl?" Sonny asked.

"Oh Sonny, I've got all these pinnies to finish for market tomorrow,"
she said. "If you can help me I might have time to look."

The sewing was difficult and he needed a lot of patience.
Luckily, Aunt Pearl was a good teacher.

By the time they had finished, there was only an hour before bed.
Everyone helped Sonny look for his homework book, but it was
nowhere to be found.

"What am I going to do? I always do my homework.
I can't go to school without it!" Sonny sighed.

"Don't be upset," said Mom. "You'll just have to explain
how busy we've been."

"Let's make sure Miss Harmston knows that we all care about your school work," she added. "I'll write a note for you as well."

On Monday, Sonny nervously gave his teacher the note.

"I'm really sorry Miss Harmston. I didn't even notice
I'd lost my homework book until Sunday lunchtime.
We looked everywhere, we really did."

He felt like he was letting
his family down.

"I believe you, Sonny,
but it's odd you didn't realize
it was lost until then," she said, smiling.
"It must have been a very busy weekend."

"It was Miss Harmston," Sonny replied, relieved.

Once they were all inside, Sonny told the whole class about his busy weekend, using his best storyteller style.

"Well, Sonny," said Miss Harmston.
"You may not have done the homework I set,
but you've done plenty of Math and English.
In fact, you've covered every other subject too."
She looked at the rest of the class.
"Who knows how?"

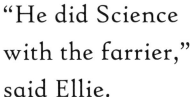

"He did Science
with the farrier,"
said Ellie.

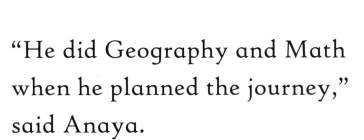

"He did Geography and Math
when he planned the journey,"
said Anaya.

"He did Music and English
at the wedding," said Bradley.

"He did Food Tech cooking lunch," said Mohammed. "And Design and Technology with Aunt Pearl."

"He did PE at the park," said Elisa.

"He did IT and History with Mrs Stevens," said Kveta.

"And Art with the community project," added Shanice.

Sonny's mouth fell open in shock.

That evening Sonny showed his family
a note from Miss Harmston.

"Who'd have thought all this home stuff
would've been school stuff too!" Dad laughed.